D.A.

D.A.

Connie Willis

Illustrated by J. K. Potter

SUBTERRANEAN PRESS 2007

First Edition

Trade Hardcover Edition
978-1-59606-120-0

Signed Limited Edition
978-1-59606-119-4

Subterranean Press
PO Box 190106
Burton, MI 48519

1.

I WAS AT SCHOOL, studying for my UCLA entrance exam and talking to Kimkim, when my phone rang.

One of Ms. Sionov's many obnoxious rules is absolute silence in the media center. "Theodora," she said, glaring at me. "You know the rules. No phones. Hand it over."

"I turned my phone off and put it in my com-pack when I came in," I told Ms. Sionov as I looked in another compartment.

"Then why is it ringing? You had your phone on and were messaging Kimkim, weren't you?"

"No," I said, which was technically true. I wasn't messaging her, I was talking to her. And the phone I was talking to her on wasn't the phone that was ringing. It's ridiculous not to let us message each other in media center, and Kimkim's a computer genius, so she rigged up a subliminal sound flatphone that goes on my wrist so I can talk to her and have it look like all I'm doing is leaning on my hand, thinking about something. "Honestly, it isn't on," I said.

"I'll bet," Ms. Sionov said, holding out her hand for the phone. "Where *is* your partner in crime today?"

"Interview at CU," I said, still searching. "It must be a schoolwide override."

"Then why isn't everyone else's phone ringing?"

Which was a good point. I dug some more and finally found the phone. "See," I said, showing her the dark screen. "I told you it was off." I hit "Display," and the words "Assembly 1 p.m. Mandatory Attendance" came up.

"I told you it was an override," I said.

Ms. Sionov grabbed the phone away from me to look, and right then Fletcher Davis's phone began to ring and then Ahmed Fitzwilliam's. And Ms. Sionov's.

She handed me my phone and ran to turn hers off. While she was gone, I forwarded Kimkim the message. "What's up?" I added, gathering up my stuff and starting for the auditorium.

"No idea," she messaged back. "Mine just rang, too. Do you think the snowboard team finally won a match?"

"That wouldn't be Mandatory Attendance." Our principal, Mr. Fuyijama, *loves* calling assemblies, to announce fire drill evacuation routes or the revised lunch schedule or the junior varsity sudoku team's taking second place at State—but those are all Optional Attendance. Assemblies to announce university acceptances and scholarships are Mandatory Attendance, but it couldn't be that. We were still in the middle of entrance-exam-and-interview season. Which was why Kimkim wasn't here.

"Can you make it back by one?" I messaged her.

"Just barely," she answered. "Save me a seat."

I maneuvered my way down the crowded hall, where everybody was asking everybody else if they knew what the assembly was about. Nobody seemed to know. "I hope it isn't the 'responsible behavior' talk," I heard Sharlanne say.

"Oh, frick," I messaged Kimkim. "Please don't let it be one of Mr. Fuyijama's speeches."

"I'll find out if it is," Kimkim messaged back. As I said, Kimkim's a computer genius. She can hack into anything, including the Euro-American

Union Department of Defense. And Mr. Fuyi-jama's daily planner.

"Thanks," I said, starting toward the girls' bathroom so I could hide out in one of the stalls if this turned out to be one of his *very long* speeches, but before I could cross the hall, Coriander Abrams came careening down the call, clutching her phone and squealing, "Ohmigod! ohmigod! A Mandatory Attendance Assembly! Theodora, do you know what that means?" She grabbed my arm and dragged me into the auditorium, squealing all the way. "This could be it! Do you think I have a chance? Tell me, honestly, do you? Isn't this ab-solutely *incred*?"

When she finally let go of me (her friend Chelsea had come up and was hugging her and shrieking, "I know it's you! Ohmigod, a cadet! You are *so* lucky!" and she had to release me so the two of them could dance around) I messaged Kimkim, "Never mind. I know what it is."

2.

I SHOULD HAVE GUESSED. I mean, the Academy's all anyone's talked about since the IASA recruiter was here last September to give her little pep talk. As if anybody at Winfrey High needed a pep talk. Three-fourths of them had already applied, and the other fourth would have if they'd thought they could pass the entrance exams. I didn't know why they even bothered sending a recruiter.

It was one of the many annoying aspects of having to go to school. I had wanted to do remote learning like everybody else, but my mom was a nostalgia freak, and she had somehow talked my dad into it.

"I thought you said you wanted me to be independent and not go along with the crowd," I'd said to him.

"I do. And what better place to do that than *in* a crowd?" he'd said, and told me a long and pointless story about the time he'd set off a stink bomb in the lunchroom.

So for the last three years I'd had to put up with Ms. Sionov's ridiculous phone rules, locker combinations, school lunches, Mandatory Attendance assemblies, and everybody drooling to get into the Academy.

It's almost impossible to do—they only take three hundred candidates a year, and less than half of them are from the Euro-American Union, so there's fierce competition. Candidates have got to score astronomically high (how appropriate!) on the Academy's entrance exams, take tons of math and science classes, be in perfect physical condition, and pass four separate levels of psychological tests and interviews.

But even that's not enough. With over fifty thousand eager applicants to choose from, IASA uses all sorts of strange formulas and extra criteria to make their picks, and nobody knows exactly what they are. The recruiter who'd come to our school had said meaningless things like, "Cadets must demonstrate dedication, determination, and devotion," and "We're looking not for excellence, but for the exceptional," and when Coriander asked her, "What can I do to improve my chances of being chosen?" she'd replied, "The Academy wants not only the *crème de la crème*, but the cream of the *crème de la crème*."

"I'd suggest you learn to milk a cow," I told Coriander.

"Oh, shut up," she'd said. "You're just jealous because I've passed the first three levels of the application process."

Some years it seems the Academy selects mostly kids who've taken astrophysics and exobiology (even though we haven't found any life anywhere out there that's bigger than a virus), and other years ethics. Or Renaissance history. Five years ago there'd been a study which seemed to indicate students in schools had a statistical edge over home- and remote-schooled, which meant everyone going to Winfrey High except me was there because they thought it would increase their chances of getting an appointment.

And, apparently, for one person, it had.

My bet was that it was Coriander. She'd taken Renaissance History *and* ethics *and* exobiology and everything else she could think of, had gone out for sports, forensics, and community service with a vengeance, and had so completely monopolized the questioning of the recruiter that I'd finally raised my hand just to shut her up for a minute.

"Yes, you have a question, Ms.—?" the recruiter asked me, smiling. She was one of those perky PR types IASA sends out.

"Baumgarten," I said. "Theodora Baumgarten. Can you explain to me why anybody in their right mind would want to go to the Academy? I mean, I know it's so you can become an astronaut and go into space, but why would anybody want to? There's no air, you're squashed into a ship the size of a juice can, and it takes years to get anywhere interesting. *If* you get there and aren't killed first by a meteor or a solar flare or a systems malfunction."

The entire student body had turned and was staring uncomprehendingly at me, as if I was speaking ancient Sumerian or something. The recruiter gave me a cold, measuring glance, and then turned and said something to Mr. Fuyijama.

"You're gonna get detention," Fletcher said.

"Any other questions?" the recruiter said, pointedly avoiding looking in my direction.

"Yes," Coriander said. "How many space engineering classes do I need to take?"

"I hope you weren't planning to apply to the Academy," Kimkim said as we left the auditorium, "because I think you just blew whatever chance you had."

"Good," I said. "I have no desire to leave *terra firma*."

"Really? You have no desire to go to the Academy at all?"

"No," I said. "Do you?"

"Of course," Kimkim said. "I mean, Mars and the rings of Saturn and all that. And getting to be a cadet. I'd love to go, but I don't have the math grades."

At that point, Coriander had stormed up and snarled, "You'd better not have ruined my chances with that little stunt," and apparently I hadn't. As we went into the auditorium now, Mr. Fuyijama beamed at her proudly from the stage.

Whoever was announcing the appointment apparently wasn't there yet. I looked for a seat way in the back in case it was the recruiter, waiting to see where Coriander and her cadre of screeching friends sat before I plunked down as far away from them as possible. I stuck my compack on the seat next to me to save it for Kimkim, who still wasn't here. She'd messaged confirmation that the assembly was indeed to announce the appointment of a cadet. "At least we won't have to listen to a speech," she said.

I wasn't so sure of that. Mr. Fuyijama was on the stage at the podium, messing with the holo-point controls and saying, "Is this on?" into the microphone. Chelsea Goodrum sat down one row in front of me, squealing into her phone.

"You know it's going to be you, Coriander! Where are you sitting?" she demanded. Apparently Coriander told her because she began to wave wildly. "Come over here!" she said. "No, there are plenty of seats!"

Oh, frick, I thought, and stood up, but the auditorium was almost full, I couldn't see two seats together anywhere except next to Chelsea, and it was too late. Mr. Fuyijama was saying, "Take your seats, students!"

I sat down, hoping Coriander hadn't had time to move either, but no, here she came with four of her shrieking friends. "This is the most incred thing ever!" Chelsea screamed, hugging her. "You're going to be a *cadet*!"

"Take your seats," Mr. Fuyijama said again, "and please turn your phones off," a totally unnecessary order since all wireless bands were automatically jammed at the beginning of every assembly.

"It's starting," I messaged Kimkim. "Where are you?"

"Denver. I'll be there in ten minutes."

"Today we're here to celebrate a tremendous honor," Mr. Fuyijama said, "the appointment of a student to the International Space Academy. Winfrey High is extremely proud to have had one of its students chosen for this honor, one of many honors over the years," and proceeded to name every single one of them. It should have sent everyone to sleep, but the whole auditorium listened intently, except for Coriander's friends, who were squeezing her arms and whispering excitedly.

"Did I miss anything?" Kimkim messaged me seven hundred and twenty-two honors later.

"No," I sent back. "Did you know Winfrey High has won the Regional Koi-Growing Contest six years running? Where are you?"

"Over by the west door. I can't get to you."

"It's just as well," I sent and told her about Coriander, who was now emitting little whimpers. "At least if you're by the door you might be able to escape."

Unlike the rest of us. Mr. Fuyijama droned on for several more geological ages and then said,

"…but none of those honors come close to the one we're here to bestow today. I'd like to welcome Admiral H.V. Washington, deputy Chief of Staff of the Space Administration."

There was thunderous applause. "Ohmigod, they sent an *admiral*!" Coriander squealed.

The admiral came over to the podium. "Every year IASA appoints candidates from all over the American-European Union to the Academy. These students have had to undergo a rigorous four-tiered application and interview process and have had to demonstrate the qualities of—"

Oh, no, not you, too, I thought. "Why don't they just give it to Coriander and put the rest of us out of our misery?" I messaged Kimkim. "Everyone knows it's her."

"Not everyone," she messaged back. "Nearly half the money's on Matt Sung."

"What do you mean, nearly half the money? Is there a pool?"

"'Betting pools are strictly forbidden at Winfrey High School,'" she quoted, mimicking Mr. Fuyijama's voice. "Of course there's a pool. Do you want to place a last-minute bet?"

"Yes," I said. "Who else is in the running besides Coriander and Matt? Tomas Rivera?"

"No, he didn't pass the second-level interview."

"You're kidding." I'd thought Tomas was a shoo-in. He had great grades, great SATs, he'd taken nationals in gymnastics.

"Our cadets, in other words," the admiral was saying, "are not just the best of the best, but the very best of the best of the best."

"Some of the sophomores are voting for Renny Nickson," Kimkim messaged.

"Renny? I thought he wanted a Rhodes."

"Not if he can get an Academy appointment instead. Nobody would turn down a chance to be a cadet. That's why the Academy announces its picks before the universities do."

"And today's appointment exemplifies that excellence," the admiral said.

It sounded like he was winding up. If I wanted in the pool, I'd better do it now. "Put me down for Matt," I said, and then glanced at Coriander. She was squeezing the hands of her friends on either side of her and biting her lip. And if sheer wanting to be a cadet was part of the criteria, she'd win it hands down. She'd been trying to get in ever since first grade. And hadn't that recruiter said something about determination and devotion? "Wait," I said. "Change my pick to Coriander."

"It gives me great pleasure to announce—"

Coriander's eyes were shut tight and she was murmuring, "Please, please, please…" and squeezing the color out of her friends' hands.

"—an appointment to the International Space Academy for—" He paused and looked straight at Coriander.

"I told you it was Coriander," I typed. Actually, this is a good thing. It means we won't have to put up with her any—"

"Theodora Baumgarten," the admiral said.

3.

THERE WAS STUNNED SILENCE, during which I had time to think, I must have heard that wrong, and then, very funny, and to look around to see who was behind this particular stink bomb.

Coriander shouted, "Theodora *Baum*garten?" and I knew he'd really said it.

"Wait," I said, and the auditorium erupted in excited applause.

Fletcher grabbed my hand and pumped it up and down. "Wow!" he shouted over the clapping. "Congratulations!"

"But—" I tried to look at my phone. "Oh, creez! Congratulations!" Kimkim's message read. "Why didn't you tell me you'd applied?"

"I didn't," I murmured, and tried to pull my

hand free so I could message her, but Chelsea grabbed it, squeezed it, and then pushed me to the end of the row. "Go on! Get down there! What are you waiting for?"

I looked down at the stage. The admiral was smiling up at me from the stage and applauding, and Mr. Fuyijama was beaming and beckoning to me. "There's been some mistake," I said, but no one was listening. They were patting and hugging me and shoving me down the steps toward the stage. "Can I touch you?" Marla Chang said in an awestruck voice, and Ms. Sionov grabbed me and kissed me. "You've always been my favorite student!" she cried.

"No, Ms. Sionov, you don't understand," I said, and then I was on the stage and Mr. Fuyijama was pumping my hand.

"Mr. Fuyijama, there's been a mistake—"

"I can't tell you how proud Winfrey High is of you!" he beamed and pushed me at the admiral, who saluted and handed me a certificate.

I read it, hoping he'd just read the name wrong, but there it was in official-looking print, "Theodora Jane Baumgarten." This can't be happening to me, I thought. "This isn't mine," I said and tried to hand the appointment back to him.

"You're supposed to salute back and say, 'Cadet Baumgarten reporting for duty,'" Mr. Fuyijama whispered.

"But I'm not—" I said. "Admiral, I didn't apply for the Academy—" and everybody must have thought I was saying, "Cadet Baumgarten reporting for duty," because they started to applaud again. The admiral shook my hand and gave me an envelope. "There's been a mistake. This isn't my—" I said, but Mr. Fuyijama was shaking my hand again and a swarm of students took the opportunity to close in around the admiral and begin bombarding him with questions.

"Mr. Fuyijama, I have to talk to you," I said. "This is all a mistake—"

"It certainly is," Coriander said, storming up. "Theodora *can't* have gotten an appointment. She didn't even take deep-field astronomy."

Mr. Fuyijama was looking at her like she was a bug, which would have been enjoyable if I hadn't been in so much trouble. "The Academy chooses for all sorts of skills," he said.

"But she can't have gotten the appointment over me," Coriander said. "She's *not* cadet material."

Mr. Fuyijama ignored her. "I've messaged your parents," he said. "They should be here any minute."

"Help," I messaged Kimkim, who I still couldn't see anywhere, and tried again with Mr. Fuyijama. "My appointment is a mistake. They mixed up the names or something."

"Don't let Coriander upset you," he said. "She was a fine candidate, but so are you, so are all of Winfrey High's students. We have one of the most outstanding schools in the country, and—"

It was hopeless. I tuned him out and looked around for the admiral. I couldn't see him anywhere. "Where did the admiral go?"

"He had to leave," Mr. Fuyijama said. "He has several more appointments to announce this afternoon."

"But I have to talk to him—" Oh, thank goodness, here was Kimkim. "Where have you *been*?" I said, pulling her off to the side of the stage. "You have to help me. Nobody will listen when I tell them there's been a mixup."

"Mixup?" she said.

"Yes, of *course* it's a mixup. I can't have been chosen. I didn't even apply to the Academy."

"You didn't?" she said happily and flung her arms around me. "Oh, I'm so glad! I thought you'd applied without telling *me*, your best friend, and I was so hurt—"

"Why would I apply? I've told you a hundred times I don't want to go into space. I want to go to UCLA."

She looked sheepish. "I know, but I thought you were just saying that because you were afraid you couldn't get in. But how could there be a mixup?"

"I don't know. Maybe there's somebody else with the same name."

"Two Theodora Baumgartens? Unlikely."

"Well, maybe there's a Theodore Baumgarten. or a Theodora Bauman. Come on, maybe we can catch the admiral before he leaves," I said, and we headed backstage.

"Wait, Theodora!" Mr. Fuyijama said before we'd gone two steps. "Your mother's here."

"I'll go see if I can catch him," Kimkim said and darted off as Mr. Fuyijama and my mom closed in on me. "I'm so *proud* of you!" she said. "I knew we made the right decision in sending you to school. You didn't want to come, remember? And now look at you, a cadet!" She and Mr. Fuyijama beamed at each other. "I still can't believe it!"

"Where's Dad?" I said. He knew I didn't want to be a cadet. He'd see this was all a ghastly mistake.

"Cheyenne," she said. "As soon as I heard, I left a message for him to come to the school. Why didn't you *tell* us you'd applied?"

"Because—"

Mr. Fuyijama patted me on the shoulder. "Shouldn't you be getting home, young lady, and getting ready to go?"

For your information, I am not going anywhere, I thought.

"What am I saying?" Mr. Fuyijama went on, smiling coyly. "You've probably had your kit all packed and ready to go for months."

"Mr. Fuyijama's right," my mom said. "We need to get you home. You only have a few hours."

"A few—?"

"I'll call your father," Mom said, steering me toward the door and away from Kimkim. "He can meet us there."

"Mom, what do you mean, a few hours?" I said, but she was talking to Dad.

"Bob? Where are you? Oh, dear. Well, turn around and go back home. We're on our way."

Kimkim appeared, shaking her head. "The admiral'd already left."

"What does my mom mean, I only have a few hours?" I asked her.

"Didn't you listen to anything the recruiter said when she was here? Cadets go straight to the Academy after they're appointed," Kimkim said, grabbing the envelope the admiral had given me and opening it. "It says they'll pick you up in exactly—oh, gosh, two hours and forty minutes."

"Let me talk to Dad," I said to Mom, who was still on the phone. Dad knew I didn't want to go into space. We'd talked about it after the recruiter came. "Hand me the phone."

Mom shook her head. "I'm talking to Grandma. You can talk to your dad when we get home. Yes, isn't it marvelous?" she said, presumably to Grandma, and then, presumably to me, "Get in the car. Yes, of *course* she'll want you to come over and say goodbye. Come on, we need to go. Goodbye, Kimkim."

"Kimkim's coming with me," I said, grabbing her arm and pushing her into the car. "She's going to help me pack."

Mom nodded absently, still talking to Grandma. She switched on the car and pulled away from the school. "Would you call Bob's parents for me? And Theodora's piano teacher? I'm sure she'll want to see her before she leaves."

"You've got to help me find out the admiral's

phone number for me," I messaged Kimkim so Mom couldn't hear what we were saying, "so I can call him and explain—"

"I'll try," she messaged back. "Academy numbers are all classified."

"Do you think I should phone Aunt Jen and Aunt Lucy?" my mom called back to me.

"*No*," I said, and Kimkim put in helpfully, "She doesn't have much time, and she's got to pack her kit, Mrs. Baumgarten."

"I suppose you're right. You should have done that beforehand, like Coriander Abrams. Her mother said she packed hers the same day she filled out her application. Oh, look," she said, pulling into the driveway, "Aunt Jen and Lucy are already here."

They were, along with Grandma, Grandpa, Grandma and Grandpa Baumgarten, and about a hundred neighbors, all holding up a big laser-spark banner twinkling, "Congratulations, Cadet Baumgarten."

The online news crews were all there, too, holding mikes, and it took me half an hour to get into the house and another fifteen minutes to escape to my room, where Kimkim was working away at my computer. "Here," she said, handing me a printout.

"What is it?" I said eagerly. "The admiral's phone number?"

"No, it's the list of what you're allowed to take. Fifteen-pound weight limit. No pets, no plants, no weapons."

"Because they know at this point I'd like to shoot them. I don't need lists," I said, throwing it in the wastebasket and going over to stand beside her. "I *need* the admiral's phone number."

"I can't get to it," Kimkim said. "I've been trying to hack into the Academy officer roster for the last half hour. It's got firewalls, moats, ramparts, the works. I'm not surprised. With fifty thousand candidates, they'd be inundated with students trying to find out the officers' numbers so they could call them and beg them to be let in, but it means I can't get in either."

"Of course you can," I said. "The database you can't hack hasn't been invented. What about calling the airport? Mr. Fuyijama said the admiral had to go announce more appointments."

"I already did. IASA refused to authorize an inflight emergency call, and the plane's onboard number is just as protected as the admiral's."

My mom poked her head in the door. "Theodora? You need to come cut your cake."

"I'm still packing," I said, grabbing my duffel bag off my closet shelf and throwing some underwear into it.

"It'll only take a minute," she said firmly. "The governor's here."

Oh, frick. "Have you heard from Dad?"

"No, but he should be here any minute. Come on. Everyone's waiting."

"I'll be right there," I said and called up Dad, but there was no answer. "I'll only be a minute," I said to Kimkim. "There has to be some kind of emergency number where we can talk to somebody. Keep trying!" and went out to the dining room.

Everyone in town was there, gathered around a sheet cake with a spaceship and silver stars spelling out "Blast off!" Mom handed me a huge piece, and I gulped it down, nodding while two dozen people I'd never seen before told me how lucky I was, and finally escaped on the pretext of taking Kimkim some cake. She waved it away, intent on her hacking, so I ate it.

"It's no use," she said. "I can't get in anywhere, IASA, the Academy cadet roster, everything's blocked."

"But there has to be a number where the cadets can call them if they've got questions."

"There is," she said, her eyes on the screen. "It's automated. Press one for a list of forbidden kit items. Press two for the Academy course schedule. Sixteen menu choices, but none for, 'if you wish to speak to an operator,' or 'I think there's been a mistake.' You don't remember the name of that recruiter, do you?"

"No. Did you check the name thing?"

"Yes. There's no Theodore Baumgarten, or Ted, or Dora. Or Bauman or Bauer or Bommgren. The closest thing I found was a Theopholus Bami, and he lives in New Delhi. And is four years old."

"Oh. I know, look up the Academy rules. Those can't be encrypted, they're public record, and there's got to be something in there about turning down an appointment."

My mom poked her head in again. "Your dad's just pulled in," she said.

Dad. Thank goodness. I waded through the crowd in the dining room again, which now seemed to contain everyone in the state of Colorado, all eating cake, and outside. "Dad, I have to talk to you. I didn't apply to the Academy—"

"You didn't?"

"No. I—"

"That's wonderful! You did just what I always told you to do—follow your own path, be independent, don't do what everybody else is doing, and look what it got you! An Academy appointment!"

"No, Dad, you don't understand. I don't want this appointment. I don't want to go to the Academy!"

"That's what you said your first day of school, remember? And do you remember what I told you?"

"The stink bomb story?"

He laughed. "No, I told you to try it for a week and then see how you felt. You're just having cold feet. When does she leave?" he asked Mom, who'd come up carrying two pieces of cake.

She handed us each one. "In twenty minutes."

"Twenty *minutes*?!" I said, looking at my digital. According to it, I still had over an hour.

"IASA called. They said they knew how eager cadets always are to go, so they're sending the escort over early."

"I have to pack," I said and shot back into my room. "You have to do something. *Now*," I told Kimkim.

"I'm trying," she said. "I looked up the Academy appointment regulations, but there's nothing in them about turning an appointment down, and

I still can't get through to anybody. I'm afraid you're going to have to go to the Academy to get this straightened out. It's the only way you're going to be able to talk to someone in person."

"I am *not* going to the Academy," I said, tossing clothes and shoes into the duffel bag she'd gotten out. "I'll hide till the escort leaves. What about your basement?"

"That won't work," she said, coming over and taking out the clothes I was putting in. "They'll think you've been kidnapped or something. Remember that cadet in Barcelona whose girlfriend tied him up so she could take his place? They'll think Coriander killed you and send out an APB. Look," she said, picking up the list and handing it to me, "you go with them and talk to whoever's in charge of admissions. I'll keep working from this end, and as soon as I've got something, I'll message you. Do your mom and dad have a lawyer?"

Mom knocked. "Theodora, your escort's here," she said.

"Give me two minutes," I shouted, frantically trying to find "3 pr. tube socks, white."

"Here's your toothbrush and toothpaste," Kimkim said, "and your phone."

"Come on, Cadet Baumgarten," my dad said, opening the door. "You don't want to keep the Academy waiting."

"Dad, what's our lawyer's name?"

"Oh, for the admission papers and things, you mean? We'll take care of all that. You just go on and have a good time." He scooped up the half-packed duffel bag and led me out through the patting, handshaking crowd to the waiting hover. "It's a good thing you didn't do what I did in high school," he said, handing me into the hover. "If you'd set off a stink bomb, they'd never have let you in."

If only I'd known, I thought. The pilot leaned across me, shut the door, and took off. I took out my phone. "Help," I messaged Kimkim.

4.

I DECIDED THERE WAS no point in trying to explain things to the pilot, especially after he said, "Boy, are you lucky! I'd sell my soul to get into the Academy!" I would just have to explain things again to the person in charge once I got there, and besides, in spite of what Kimkim had said, I was seriously considering making a run for it when he let me out at the gates, but he landed me inside the high, razor-wire-tipped walls and walked me into the main building past two heavily armed sentries and handed me over to a man in an IASA uniform.

"I want to talk to the person in charge of admissions," I said to him.

"Name?"

"Theodora Baumgarten," I said, hoping against hope it wasn't on his list, but he found it immediately, handed me an ID badge, and weighed my bag.

"You're two pounds over," he said, opening it and taking out my phone. "You can get rid of this. It won't work in the Academy."

Oh, frick, I hadn't considered that possibility. I'd have to message Kimkim and tell her—

"I have a sentimental attachment to it," I said. "You can take my curling iron instead."

The door behind us opened and two girls came in.

"Oh, look at this! I can't believe we're here!" one of them said, clutching her chest just like Coriander, and the other one kept repeating, "Ohmigod, ohmigod, ohmigod!" till I thought she was going to hyperventilate.

"You're still overweight," the IASA guy said. "You sure you don't want to give up your phone?"

"I'm sure," I said, pulling out my iPod and some DVDs.

He shrugged. "Suit yourself," he said, handed me back the bag and turned to the Hyperventilator. "Name?"

"Excuse me," I said, moving back in front of her. "I asked to see the person in charge of admissions."

"You'll have to talk to your sector officer," he said looking at the list. "H-level. Second elevator on the right."

I took it down to H, messaging Kimkim the news about the phone on the way down. "Working on it," she answered immediately, so at least the phone worked in this part of the Academy. They must just jam the student areas, which meant till Kimkim found a way around it, I'd have to sneak off to an area where it did work.

If I was here that long. Which I might be, since the fourth-year cadet waiting for me on H-level looked at me totally blankly when I told him I wanted to see the admissions person.

"Never mind," I said. "Take me to the head of the Academy."

"You mean the Commander?"

"Yes," I said firmly.

"This way," he said, and led me down a long cement corridor, up an even longer ramp, and into another elevator. He pushed three, and we went up for a very long way. It opened on an accordion-pleated tunnel, like a jetway, ending in a narrow, curved corridor lined with doors.

He stopped in front of one of them, opened it

and stepped aside so I could enter. "Is this the Commander's office?" I asked.

"No. Wait here," he said and walked away, and before I could start after him, the Hyperventilator had swooped down on me.

"Isn't this exciting?" she squealed. "Come on!" She grabbed my arm and dragged me into the room, which was clearly not the Commander's office. It was a room the size of a closet with curved walls and two bunks. "I can't believe we're in the same cabin!"

Cabin—?

She'd plopped down on the lower bunk. "Come on, get strapped in! We launch in five minutes! Aren't we lucky?" she said, busily fastening straps. "All the other classes had to spend their first semester earthside before they got to go up."

The elevators, the jetway, the curving corridor— "We're in a *spaceship*?" I said, calculating whether I could make it down that jetway to the elevator in two minutes.

"I know, I can't believe it's happening either!"

An alarm began to sound. "All cadets to their acceleration couches." I dived for the remaining bunk.

"You do the chest straps first," the Hyperventilator said. "Just think, in a few hours we'll be on the Ra!"

"The Ra?" I said, struggling with the straps. They were so in love with the Academy, they'd named it after a god?

"That's what cadets call the Academy space station, the *Robert A. Heinlein*. The *RAH*, get it? And now we're cadets! Can you *believe* this is actually happening?"

"No."

"Me neither!" she said. "Don't you think you'd better put your emesis bag on?"

5.

I THREW UP ALL the way to the *RAH*.

"Gosh, I didn't think it was possible to throw up at 4g's," the Hyperventilator said. "Maybe you'll feel better when we go into freefall."

I didn't. I went through my vomit bag and hers and threw up on the bunk, the walls, the Hyperventilator, and, once we were weightless, on the air in front of me, where it formed disgusting-looking yellowish-brown globules that floated around the cabin for the rest of the trip.

"What on earth did you eat?" the Hyperventilator asked.

"Cake," I said miserably and vomited again.

"It can't last much longer," she said, ducking a large globule floating toward her. "You can't have anything left."

Also not true.

"You'll be okay once we get to the *RAH*," she said.

"Rah, rah, rah," I said weakly and proved her wrong by throwing up all over the cadet sent to unstrap us, on the connecting deck, and the airlock.

At least *this* will convince them there's been a mistake, I thought, as the cadet half-carried me to my quarters, but he said cheerfully, "A touch of space sickness, huh?" He lowered me onto my bunk. "Happens to every cadet."

"I'm *not* a cadet," I said, and then, even though I wanted to lie there in my bunk and die, said, "I want to see the Commander."

"I know how you feel," he said. "My first day up here I wanted to go home, too. You'll feel better after a shower and a nap."

"No, I won't. I demand to see the head. Now," I said and got up to show him I was serious, but the minute I did, I felt wildly lightheaded and on the verge of toppling, as if I were in a canoe about to tip over.

"Coriolus effect," he said, grabbing my arm and lowering me back onto the bunk. "It takes a couple of days to get used to."

"I won't live that long," I muttered, and he laughed again.

"I need to go get the other cadets settled in, and then I'll come back and see how you're doing," he said, covering me up with a Mylar blanket. "If you need me before that, just hit send." He handed me a communicator. "And don't worry. A little thing like spacesickness won't get you thrown out of the Academy."

"But I want to be—" I began, but he was already gone, and the thought of getting up off the bunk to go after him, or even of pressing the button on the communicator, sent the room toppling over again.

I'll just lie here very, very quietly till he comes back, I thought, and then insist on seeing the Commander, but I must have been asleep when he came back, because when I opened my eyes, the Hyperventilator was unpacking her kit on the other bunk. "Oh, good, you're awake," she said. "We're going to be bunkmates! Isn't that incred! I'm Libby, I mean, Cadet Thornburg. Are you feeling better?"

"No," I said, though I was, a little. At least I was able to sit up. However, when I tried to stand, the room gave a sudden lurch, and I had to grab for the wall, and it, the other walls, and Libby seemed to be leaning ominously toward me. I reared back and nearly fell over.

"It's because of the Coriolus effect from the spin on the space station. It makes everything seem to tilt toward you. Isn't it incred?"

"Umm," I said. "How long does it take to get used to it?" It must not be that long. She was moving around without any trouble. Or maybe that was one of the things IASA tested for in their four-tiered screening process.

"I don't know. I wanted to get a head start," she said, stowing clothes in the locker above her bunk, "so I practiced in an artificial-gravity simulator before I came. Three weeks, maybe?"

I would never last three weeks. Which meant I had to get in to see the Commander now. I pressed the communicator button and then spent the time till the fourth-year got there working on standing up, walking over to the door, and fighting the urge to grab onto something, anything, at all times.

The fourth-year looked surprised to see me on my feet. I told him I wanted to see the Commander, "Don't you want to wait till you feel steadier?" he asked, looking at my vomit-spattered clothes. "And have a chance to clean up?"

"No."

"Okay," he said doubtfully. "What did you want to see the Commander about?"

If I told him, he'd stare blankly at me or say everyone with spacesickness felt that way. "There's a problem with my application," I said.

"Oh, then, you want the registrar."

"No, I—" I began and then decided the registrar was exactly who I wanted to see. He'd have the applications on file, and when he saw I didn't have one, he could correct the mistake immediately. "Okay, take me to the registrar's office."

"That's not necessary," he said. "You can message him from here." He switched on the terminal above my bunk.

"No," I said. "I want to see him in person."

"Okay, wait here, and I'll see if he's available."

"No," I said, letting go of the wall with an effort. "I'm coming with you."

It was the longest walk of my life. I couldn't seem to overcome the feeling that everything, including the fourth-year, was about to pitch forward onto me and/or that I was about to float away, and I periodically had to latch onto handgrips and/or the fourth-year in spite of myself.

"It's because the gravity's only two-thirds that of earth," he said. "You'll get used to it. You're lucky it's not a full g. The more rotation, the more Coriolus effect. Any less, though, and there's bone loss. Two-thirds is a happy medium."

"That's what you think," I muttered, showing no signs of getting used to it, even though he led me through what seemed like miles of tube-like corridors and locks and ladders, ending finally in an office not much bigger than my cabin. A guy who looked like my dad was seated at a console.

"What can I do for you, Cadet Baumgarten?" he asked kindly.

I poured out my whole story, hoping against hope he wouldn't give me another of those I-don't-understand-what-language-you're-speaking looks.

He didn't. He said, "Oh, dear, that's terrible. I can't imagine how that could have happened."

Relief flooded over me.

"I'll look into this immediately. Cadet Apley," he called into an inner office, "find me Cadet Baumgarten's file." He turned back to me. "Don't worry. We'll get this straightened out."

A young woman's voice called out to him, "The files for the new cadets haven't been transmitted yet, sir."

"Well, tell them I need them as soon as possible."

"Yes, sir," she said.

"Don't worry, Cadet Baumgarten," he said. "We'll get this straightened out. I intend to launch a full investigation." He stood up and extended his hand. "I'll notify you as soon as we've determined what happened."

I ignored his hand. "How long will that be?"

"Oh, it shouldn't take more than a week or two."

"A *week* or two?" I said. "But you've made a mistake. I'm not supposed to be here."

"If that is the case, you'll of course be sent home immediately," he said, showing me the door. "In the meantime, may I congratulate you on your rapid adaptation to artificial gravity. Very impressive."

If I could have thrown up on him, I would have, but there was no cake left. Instead, I planted myself in front of him as firmly as was possible in two-thirds g and said, "I want to make a phone call."

"Cadets aren't allowed phone calls for the first two weeks of term. After that, you can make one two-minute earthside call a month," he said.

"I know my rights," I said, trying not to sway. "Prisoners are allowed a phone call."

He looked amused. "The *RAH* is not a prison."

Wanna bet? "It's my legal right," I said stubbornly. "A *private* phone call."

He sighed. "Cadet Apley," he called into the inner office, "set up a Y49TDRS link for Cadet Baumgarten," and handed me a satellite phone. "Two minutes. There'll be a six-second lag. This will count as next month's call," he said and went into the inner office and shut the door.

They were probably listening in, but I didn't care. I called Kimkim. "I'm so sorry," she said. "I didn't know they were taking cadets straight up to the *Heinlein*. Are you okay?"

"No," I said. "Did you find out my mom and dad's lawyer's name?"

Seconds passed, and then she said, "Yes, I talked to her."

"What did she say?"

More seconds. "That an Academy appointment was considered a legally-binding contract."

Oh, frick.

"So I went online and found a lawyer who specializes in Academy law."

"And?" Creez, this lag was maddening.

"He said he only handled cases of cadets who'd been eliminated from the Academy and were trying to get reinstated. He said he couldn't find any record of a case where a cadet had wanted *out*."

"Did he say how these cases he handled *got* eliminated?" I asked, thinking maybe I could do whatever it was they did.

"Failing their courses, mostly," she said. "But, listen, don't do anything that might mess up your chances at UCLA. That's why these cadets file lawsuits, because flunking out of the Academy pretty much ruined their chances at getting into any other university."

Worse and worse. "Listen, you've got to figure out some way we can talk." I told her about the one call a month.

"I'll see what I can do. They didn't take your phone away from you, did they?"

"No," I said.

"Did they say anything about how this call worked?"

"They called it a Y49TDRS, whatever that is."

"It means it's relayed through tracking, data, and relay satellites," she said. "A Y49 shouldn't be too hard to patch onto, but it may take—"

There was a buzz. "Call over," an automated voice said.

6.

I SPENT THE NEXT day and a half checking my phone for messages and hoping Kimkim hadn't been about to say, "It may take months for me to come up with something," or, worse, "It may take extensive modifications to your phone's circuits," and worrying that if the registrar had been listening in, it didn't matter. They'd jam whatever Kimkim tried.

Then classes started, and I spent every waking moment trying to keep up with cadets who'd not only taken astrogation and exobotany, but knew how to dock a shuttle, read a star chart, and brush their teeth while weightless. First-year cadets had to spend half of each watch in the non-rotated sections of the *RAH*, learning to live and work in microgravity. Most of them (including, of course, Libby) had taken classes in weightlessness on earth, and the rest had clearly been chosen for their ability to float from one end of the module to the other without crashing into something, a gene I obviously lacked. The second day I sneezed, did a backward triple somersault, and crashed into a bank of equipment, an escapade that gave me the idea of pleading a bad cold and asking to see the doctor—a medical discharge surely couldn't hurt my chances at UCLA—but when I went to the infirmary, the medic said, "Stuffiness in the head is a normal side effect of weightlessness," and gave me a sinus prescription.

"What about chronic vertigo?" I asked. I was actually down to only a couple of episodes a day, but it had occurred to me that "inability to tolerate space environment" might be a way out.

"If it hasn't disappeared a month from now, come see me," he said and sent me back to EVA training. Luckily, I didn't sneeze during my spacewalk and go shooting off into space, but being outside and linked to the *RAH* only by a thin tether reminded me just how dangerous space was.

Well, that, and the fact that those dangers were the second favorite topic of the cadets at mess and during rec periods. If they weren't talking about the difficulty of detecting fires in a weightless environment (there aren't any flames, just a hard-to-see reddish glow), they were recounting gruesome tales of jammed oxygen lines and carbon monoxide buildup and malfunctioning heating units that froze students into cadet-sicles. Or speculating on all the things that *might* happen, from unexpected massive solar flares to killer meteors to explosive decompression. All of which made it clear I needed to get off of here *soon*. I messaged the registrar during my study period, but he said he was still waiting for the cadet files.

There was still no word from Kimkim. I checked my phone every time I had the chance and tried to send her periodic *Maidez*'s, but each time the display said, "Number out of range," which was putting it mildly.

I messaged the registrar again. Still waiting.

You're still waiting? I thought. At least he had an office of his own. He didn't have to share with Miss Ohmigod, This Is So Incred! Libby adored everything about the Academy—the sardine-can cabins, the rehydrated food, the exhausting schedule of lectures and labs and exercise and freefall training. She even loved the falling-off-a-log vertigo. "Because then you know you're really in space!"

And she wasn't the worst one. Several of the cadets acted like they were in a cathedral, wandering the corridors with their mouths open and speaking in hushed, reverent tones. When I mentioned that the place smelled like a gym locker, they looked at me like I was committing heresy, and went back to the cadets' favorite topic of conversation, how *lucky* they were to be here. By the end of a week I was ready to walk through an airlock without a spacesuit just to get away from them.

I was also worried about how I was going to talk to Kimkim if and when she figured out a phone connection, and about finding a safe place to stash my phone so the registrar couldn't suddenly confiscate it. I checked the *RAH*'s schematics, but there was nowhere a person could go to be alone on the entire space station. Every classroom and lab was used every hour of every watch, so were the mess, the gym, and the weightless modules, and when I'd gone to the infirmary, there hadn't been separate examining rooms, just a tier of cots.

There was temporary privacy in the shower, (very temporary—water is even more limited than the phone call times) and there was supposed to be "private time" half an hour before lights-out, but it wasn't enforced, and Libby's half of the cabin was always crammed with cadets discussing how *exciting* it had been to learn to use the zero-g toilet. I began to actually miss Coriander.

I checked the schematics again, looking for anything at all that might work. The inner room of the registrar's office might in a pinch, though when I'd gone over to ask him what was taking the files so long, I'd been told the section was off-limits to first-years. So was the docking module, and all the outer sections were exposed to too much radiation to make them practical.

The only other possibility was the storage areas, which in the super-compact world of the *RAH* meant every space that wasn't being used for something else—floors, ceilings, walls, even the airlocks. The diagrams showed all those spaces as filled with supplies, but it occurred to me (during a private-time discussion about the joys of learning to sit down in two-thirds g) that once those supplies had been used, the place they'd been might be empty.

I noted some of the possible spots and for the next few days spent my rest period exploring, and finally came up with a space between the plastic drums of nutrients for the hydroponics farm. It wasn't very big, and it was above the ceiling, but luckily it was in the freefall area, and I'd finally figured out how to propel myself from one location to another in it without major damage. I half-drifted, half-rappelled my way up (over?) to the ceiling, squeezed into the space (which turned out to be a perfect size, big enough, but too small to drift around in), replaced the hatch, and spent a blissful fifteen minutes alone.

It would have been longer, but I remembered a class was scheduled to come in sometime soon, and I couldn't afford to get caught. When I got back to my cabin, I memorized the freefall-area use schedule and checked for a message from the registrar.

There wasn't one, but on my schedule was "Conference Registrar's office. Tuesday. 1600 hours." Which meant I wouldn't need a hiding place after all.

7.

"I'VE GONE OVER YOUR application," the registrar said, "and everything appears to be in order."

"In order?" I said blankly.

"Yes," he said, looking at the console. "Application, entrance exams, endurance test results, psychological battery scores. It's all here."

"Application?" I said, standing up too fast and nearly shooting over the desk at him. "I told you, I didn't apply!"

"I also sent for the interviewer assessments and the minutes of the selection committee. You did in fact apply—"

"I did *not*—"

"—and were duly appointed."

"I want to see that application. It must be

a forgery—"

"Conflicted feelings among new cadets are not unusual. A strange new environment, separation from family, performance anxiety can all be factors. Did you perhaps have a friend who also wanted to get into the Academy?"

"Yes, but…I mean, *she* wanted in the Academy, I didn't. I didn't—"

He nodded sagely. "And now you feel by accepting your appointment you're betraying that friend—"

"*No*," I said. "I did not write that application. Let me see it."

"Certainly," he said, hit several keys, and the image of the application came up on the screen.

"Theodora Jane Baumgarten," it read. This is like a bad dream, I thought. Birthdate, address, school… Before I could read the rest of it, the registrar had hit the next screen and the next. "You see?" he said, blanking the last screen before I could get a good look at it. "And quite an impressive application, if I may say so. I think you'll make an excellent addition to the Academy."

"I want to see the Commander," I said.

"She'd only tell you the same thing." He hit several more keys, and the terminal spat out a slip of paper. "I've made an appointment for you with Dr. Tumali. He'll help you sort out any conflicting feelings you—"

"I don't *have* any conflicting feelings. I *hate* this place, and I want to go home," I screeched at him and stormed out, slamming the door behind me. Well, sort of. Slams aren't terribly impressive at two-thirds g, and after I'd done it, I realize I should have demanded another phone call instead, this one to my mother. She'd said she'd secretly hoped I'd apply. Maybe she'd decided to do it for me. Or maybe Coriander had, as some kind of hideous joke. Or Mr. Fuyijama. The more cadets he had, the better Winfrey High looked.

But even if they'd filled out an application and forged my signature, they couldn't have faked the entrance exams or the interview. It made no sense, and I had no time to think about it. I had an essay due on asteroid mining and a lunar geography exam to study for. "Help," I messaged Kimkim.

The display lit up. "Number out of range."

8.

THREE DAYS LATER, WHEN I had decided I was going to have to do something drastic to get myself expelled, and forget UCLA, my phone rang in the middle of rest period. "What was that?" Libby said drowsily.

"A killer meteor," I said, switching the phone to "message."

"Are you there?" the display read.

"Yes," I messaged, "hang on," and took off at a run for the freefall area. And nearly got caught by a group of second-years playing weightless soccer. I had to wait till they'd finished and left to swing up to my hiding place, hoping Kimkim hadn't concluded she'd lost me in the meantime.

As soon as I was inside the space, I switched the phone to "voice," and said, "Kimkim, are you there?"

There was no answer. Oh, Frig, I thought, and then remembered the lag.

"I'm here," she said. "Sorry I took so long. I had trouble setting up an encryption so the Academy can't eavesdrop on us."

"That's okay," I said. "I need you to get a look at my Academy application."

"I thought you said you didn't apply."

"I *didn't*, but the registrar showed me something that looked like one. I need you to find out what kind of signature verification it's got on it, an R-scan or a thumbprint, and what site notarized it."

"You think IASA faked it?"

"IASA or somebody else. You didn't submit an application in my name, did you?"

"I resent that," she said. "If I was going to fake one, I'd have faked my own."

She called back two days later in the middle of tensor calculus to tell me she couldn't get to my application. "I was finally able to hack into the Academy's database and the cadet applications files, but I can't get into yours."

"Because it doesn't exist," I said after I got to my hiding place.

"No, I mean, there's a file with your name on it, but I can't get access."

"What about having someone they won't connect with me make the request?"

"I already tried that. I used my sister's friend's friend in Jakarta. She couldn't get in either. Neither could any of the professional hackers I contacted. It's blocked. I can get into the other applications, but not yours."

"Well, keep trying," I said and hung up. I stuck the phone down the front of my uniform, crawled over to the hatch, and began to slide it open.

And heard voices below me.

The soccer players weren't supposed to be in here till 1900 hours. I slid the hatch silently shut and flattened myself against it, listening. "It's my bunkmate," Libby was saying. "I've *tried* to be friends with her, but she acts like she doesn't want to be here."

You're right, I thought. In more ways than one.

"Libby's right, her bunkmate's got a terrible attitude," one of her friends said. "I have no idea how she got appointed when there are thousands of candidates who'd *love* to be here."

"I know the Academy must have had a good reason for picking her," Libby said, "but..." and launched into a ten-minute list of my shortcomings which I had no choice but to lie there and listen to. "That's why I asked you to meet me here," she said when she was finally finished. "I need your advice."

"Tell the dean you want a different bunk-mate," another friend said.

"I can't," Libby said. "Inability to foster healthy personal relations is the number one reason for failing first-year."

"Cut her EVA tether next time she's outside," the first friend said, which didn't exactly sound like fostering healthy personal relations to me.

"Maybe you should introduce her to Cadet Griggs," another voice said. "It sounds like they'd be perfect for each other."

"Who's Cadet Griggs?" Libby asked.

"He's a third-year in my exochem class. Jeffrey Griggs. He doesn't like anything or anybody."

"I sat next to him in mess last week, and he was completely insufferable," the first one said. "And conceited. He claims he didn't even have to apply to get in. He—what was that?"

I must have kicked one of the nutrient drums in my surprise. I held my breath, praying they didn't investigate.

"He claims he was so brilliant they just ap-pointed him without his taking any entrance exams or anything."

"You should definitely introduce them, Libby, and maybe they'll move in together, and your problem will be solved, and so will hers."

My problem *is* solved, I thought.

As soon as they left, I called Kimkim. "I need you to get into the cadet application files."

"I told you, I can't get anywhere near your application."

"Not mine," I said. "Cadet Jeffrey Griggs'. He's a third-year."

She said the name back to me. "What am I looking for?"

"The application," I said.

She called back the next day. "There's no application on file for Jeffrey Griggs."

I knew it. Listen, I need you to go through all the cadet files for the last five years and see how many others are missing."

"I already did. I went back eight years and found four more, one last year, two four years ago, one seven."

"I need you to find out where they are now."

"I did, and you're not going to like the answer. All but one of them are still in the Academy or working for IASA."

"What about the one who isn't?"

"Medical discharge. 'Inability to tolerate space environment.' Her name's Palita Duvai. She's in graduate school at Harvard," Kimkim said. "Do you want their names?"

"Yes," I said, even though I knew the registrar would say five missing applications didn't prove anything. He'd claim they'd been accidentally erased, and if it wasn't an accident, then why hadn't they posted phony applications like the one they'd shown me? I asked Kimkim that.

"I don't know," she said, "but it's definitely not an accident. When I looked up their IASA assignments, I found something else. Next to their ranks are the letters 'DA.' It's part of Jeffrey's class rank, too—'Third-year Cadet, DA.'"

DA. District Attorney? Didn't Apply? Dragged Away Kicking and Screaming?

"I looked it up in the IASA lexicon, but it wasn't there," she said. "Do you want me to try to find out what it stands for?"

"I don't think that will be necessary," I said. I signed off, went back to my cabin and got the slip of paper the registrar had given me with the psychiatrist appointment on it, wrote "DA" on the back, and took it up. I handed it, folded, to one of the guards, told him to slide it under the registrar's door, and went back to my cabin to wait.

I didn't even make it halfway. A fourth-year cadet was waiting for me before I even reached the dorm section. "Cadet Baumgarten?" she said. "The registrar wants to see you," and took me back up to his office.

"Come in, Ms. Baumgarten," the registrar said. "Sit down." I noted that the slip of paper was on his desk.

"The cadet said the Commander wanted to—" I began and then absorbed what he'd said. Ms. Baumgarten, not Cadet Baumgarten. I sat down.

"I'm sorry to have taken so long getting back to you," he said. "The first few weeks of term are always so hectic. However, I wanted to tell you that we've completed the check on your application, and you were correct. A mistake in our admissions software wrongly identified you as a candidate. The IASA sincerely regrets the error and any inconvenience it may have caused you."

"Inconvenience—!"

"You will be reimbursed for that inconvenience and your lost classtime," he went on smoothly. "I understand you want to go to UCLA. We've already spoken to them and explained the situation, and they've agreed to reschedule your interview at your convenience. If you encounter any other problems, feel free to contact me." He handed me a folder. "Here are your discharge papers."

I opened the folder and read the papers. Next to "Reason for Discharge," it read, "Medical— Inability to Tolerate Space Environment."

"You're free to leave whenever you wish," the registrar said. "We've reserved a space for you on tomorrow's shuttle. It leaves at 0900 hours. Or, if you prefer, we'd be happy to arrange for a civilian shuttle, and if there's anything else we can do, please let us know."

He stood up and came around the desk. "I hope your time with us hasn't been too unpleasant," he said and extended his hand.

And all I had to do was shake it, go pack my kit, and get on that shuttle, and I'd be back on blessed Earth and on my way to UCLA. It was extremely tempting.

"Sorry," I said, folding my arms across my chest. "Not good enough."

"Not—? If you're worried about questions from your friends and family regarding your leaving the Academy, I'll be happy to issue a statement explaining that inner-ear problems made it impossible for you to adjust to the Coriolus effect. Medical discharges carry no stigma—"

"I don't want a medical discharge. I want to know the truth. Why did you hijack me? And how many people have you done it to besides me? I know of at least ten," I lied. "What do you want with us? And don't tell me you don't have enough candidates."

"Actually, that's exactly why we hijacked you," he said, and called into the inner office. "Commander! I think you'd better take over!"

The Commander came in. At least, she was wearing a commander's uniform and insignia, but she couldn't be the Commander. She was the recruiter who'd come to Winfrey High. "Hello, Ms. Baumgarten," she said. "It's nice to see you again."

"You!" I said. "You kidnapped me because of that question I asked in assembly, to punish me."

"Yes and no," she said. "Punishment was the furthest thing from my mind. And I prefer the word 'shanghaied' to 'kidnapped.'"

"Shanghaied?"

"Yes. It comes from the practice in the port of Shanghai in the 1800s of ships' captains' using unorthodox methods for obtaining crews for long, dangerous voyages. When they couldn't get the sailors they needed any other way, they drugged them, carried them aboard, and held them prisoner till they were out to sea. Not a nice technique, but sometimes necessary."

"I don't believe you," I said. "You have thousands and thousands of people who are dying to go to the Academy every year."

"You're right," she said. "Last year we had nine thousand students who successfully completed all four tiers of the screening policy. From those, we chose three hundred, which meant they were the most determined and dedicated of those nine thousand."

"And every one of them's *thrilled* to be here," I said.

"Exactly. They love the Academy, they love IASA, and that sort of intense devotion is absolutely necessary. Space exploration is an impossibly challenging and dangerous, often deadly, undertaking. Without complete belief in what they're doing, it couldn't be done. But that sort of devotion can also be a handicap. Explorers who are too in love with the jungle end up being bitten by snakes or eaten by tigers. To survive, IASA has to have people who are fully aware of the jungle's dangers and disadvantages and not the least enchanted by its beauties.

"Which means, along with astrogation and the ability to live in confined quarters, we also recruit for skepticism, independence, and questioning of authority—in short, for people who don't like the jungle.

Unfortunately, those people generally do everything they can to avoid it, which is why we are forced to—"

"Shanghai people," I said. "Let me get this straight, the reason you wanted me to come to the Academy was because I didn't want to?"

"Yes."

"And what was I supposed to do here?"

"Precisely what you did. Refuse to be impressed, challenge authority, break the rules. Your determination to communicate with your friend was particularly educational. We obviously need to do a much better job of preventing hacking. Also, we've learned not to put DA even on interior records. And it's clear we need to reexamine the necessity of providing private space for our cadets. You've performed a valuable service," she said. "IASA thanks you." She extended her hand.

"I'm not done asking questions yet," I said. "Why do you have to shanghai people? Why didn't you just *ask* me?"

"Would you have come?"

I thought about that day she'd come to Winfrey High to recruit applicants. "No."

"Exactly," she said. "Besides, bringing DAs here involuntarily ensures the critical mindset we're looking for."

"It also ensures that when they find out, they'll be so furious they won't want to have anything to do with the Academy or IASA," I said.

"True," she said ruefully, "but they don't usually find out. You're only the second one."

"Was the first one Palita Duvai?" I asked.

"No," she said. "Unfortunately, Cadet Duvai's medical discharge was real. Inner ear complications."

But if she wasn't the one, I thought, frowning, then that meant uncovering the conspiracy didn't automatically mean a discharge, and that meant—

"The other DAs either concluded there'd been a bureaucratic foul-up or that they'd been so outstanding they hadn't needed to apply," she said.

Jeffrey Griggs, I thought.

"Or they eventually gave up trying to go home and decided that, in spite of the food and the solar flares, they liked the Academy." She shook her head. "I underestimated your dislike of space. And your friend's hacking and communication abilities. Tell me, is Kimkim interested in becoming a cadet?"

"That depends on what you're recruiting for," I said. "If you want a great hacker, yes. If you're looking for another DA, then no, definitely not, she'd probably have to be dragged up here kicking and screaming. And the sooner the better."

The Commander grinned. "I really am sorry to lose you. I think you would have made an excellent DA." She leaned back. "Have we answered all your questions?"

"No," I said. "I have two more."

"You want to know what DA stands for?"

"No, I already know that. Devil's advocate."

She looked at the registrar. "I told you she was good." She smiled back at me. "You want to know who the other cadet was who figured out what had happened."

"No, I know that, too. It was you."

She nodded.

"Did you decide you liked the Academy in spite of its shortcomings?" I asked.

"No," she said. "I thought it was a complete mess, and that if they didn't get some people in charge who knew what they were doing, and change things, it was going to fall completely apart."

"I think you're right," I said. "You've got to get some private space on board before somebody kills somebody, and surely something can be done about the food. And you've got to get a lot more cadets with computer skills up here."

"We'll see what we can do," the Commander said and extended her hand. "Welcome aboard."

I saluted her. "Cadet Baumgarten reporting for duty," I said.

"You said you had two questions," the registrar said. "What was the other one?"

"Which of you won the pool?"

"I did," the Commander said and grinned at the registrar. "I *told* you she was good."

Yes, well, they don't know how good. Or how much trouble they're letting themselves in for. If it's independence, questioning authority, and bending the rules they want, Kimkim and I can come up with all kinds of stuff. I went straight to my hiding place and called her.

The display lit up. "Illegal transmission," it read. "Not allowed."

I waited, and in a couple of minutes Kimkim said, "Sorry. It took me awhile to route around their jamming devices. I found out what DA stands for."

"So did I," I said. "I definitely think you should reconsider applying for the Academy. And I think it would be a good idea to pack your kit now so you won't have to do it at the last minute."

"I already did," she said.

"Good," I said. "I've got a list of stuff I need you to bring when you come up. First, I want you to ask my dad for his stink bomb formula..."